Postman Pat's Secret Special Delivery

Illustrations by Niall Harding

EGMONT

EGMONT

We bring stories to life

First published in Great Britain 2012 by Egmont UK Limited
The Yellow Building, 1 Nicholas Road, London W11 4AN

Postman Pat® © 2012 Woodland Animations Ltd, a division of Classic Media Limited.
Licensed by Classic Media Distribution Limited. Original writer John Cunliffe.
Royal Mail and Post Office imagery is used by kind permission of Royal Mail Group PLC.
All rights reserved.

ISBN 978 1 4052 5055 9

46796/3

Printed in Italy

Egmont is passionate about helping to preserve the world's remaining ancient forests.
We only use paper from legal and sustainable forest sources.

This book is made from paper certified by the Forest Stewardship Council® (FSC®),
an organisation dedicated to promoting responsible management of forest resources.
For more information on the FSC, please visit www.fsc.org. To learn more about
Egmont's sustainable paper policy, please visit www.egmont.co.uk/ethical

There's a treasure hunt and Postman Pat must deliver the prize to a secret location! Will Postman Pat be able to prove that no job is too tricky for the Special Delivery Service?

It was a sunny day in Pencaster. Postman Pat had just arrived at the mail centre.

Ben, the general manager, waved Postman Pat over to the office.

"Ooh, what have you got there?" asked Postman Pat.

"Ssshh!" said Ben. "This special delivery is top secret, Pat."

Ben brought out a beautiful tepee.

"Lauren has organised a treasure hunt for the children," said Ben. "The tepee is for a surprise sleepover at the end!"

"The children will love that!" said Postman Pat. "Where am I taking it?"

Ben handed Postman Pat the directions. "You must keep the location a secret."

"You can trust us!" Pat smiled. But as Jess jumped up to see the tepee, he knocked the directions into the paper shredder!

Over at the town square, Reverend Timms had gathered the children together.

"Welcome to the treasure hunt!" he said. "Are you ready for your first clue?"

"Yes! Yes!" the children chorused, excitedly.

Reverend Timms held up a picture of a light bulb. The children all started whispering and ran off to solve the clue!

Meanwhile, Postman Pat was having trouble finding out where to take the tepee.

Lauren was waiting at the secret location. But when Pat tried to ring her mobile phone, he couldn't get through.

"I'll have to do the treasure hunt myself!" said Postman Pat. "The clues will lead me to Lauren."

Postman Pat loaded the tepee into the van and sped off to find the first clue.

Reverend Timms was very surprised to see Postman Pat on the treasure hunt.

"I need to deliver the prize to the end," Postman Pat explained. "But I don't know where the finish is!"

Reverend Timms showed Postman Pat the light bulb clue.

"Hmm . . . street lamps, shop lights, traffic lights . . . " said Pat. Then he had a thought. "The lighthouse!"

When Postman Pat arrived at the lighthouse, Bill Thompson and Lucy Selby were already there.

"I can't reach it!" Bill said, jumping up.

The second clue was stuck on the lighthouse. It was a picture of a carrot.

"Michael sells carrots!" Bill said. "Let's go!"

"Wait!" said Postman Pat. But Bill had already disappeared over the square.

By the time Postman Pat arrived at Michael's shop, the children had already seen the next clue and left.

"You're a bit old for a treasure hunt, Pat!" smiled Michael.

"It's a long story!" replied Postman Pat.

The third clue was a picture of a rocket.

"The Greendale Rocket!" said Postman Pat. "The clue must be at the station!"

Postman Pat and Jess sped over to Pencaster Station, racing past the children on the way!

Ajay had stuck a huge picture of a woolly sheep on the side of the train.

"There's one place I know to find sheep," Pat said. "Thompson Ground! Bye, Ajay!"

But when Postman Pat started up his van, it began to splutter. The engine had overheated!

While Postman Pat was stuck at the station, the children raced ahead.

The final clue was a picture of a sail. Ted Glenn was taking the children to the secret location by boat.

"All aboard now!" Ted said. "The prize is on the island."

"I wish my dad could see me!" said Julian.

But Postman Pat was nowhere in sight.

Lauren and Amy had just finished putting the final touches to the picnic. Amy had even built a campfire for the sleepover.

"The children should be here any minute now!" Amy said, excitedly.

"Yes, but we're still waiting for the tepee!" Lauren said, worried. "I wonder what's taking Pat so long?"

Postman Pat finally fixed his van. But when he arrived at the jetty, the children were already sailing across the lake!

"We've missed the boat!" cried Postman Pat.

Then Jess jumped into an old rowing boat in the water. Using the tepee as a sail, they quickly sailed off towards the island.

The children all waved in surprise as Postman Pat and Jess went sailing by!

Postman Pat finally reached the island.

"We made it!" he said, happily.

Postman Pat quickly put up the tepee, just as the children ran on to the island. They all cheered when they saw the prize tepee!

"You missed an amazing treasure hunt, Dad," said Julian, excitedly.

"Why don't you tell me all about it?" Postman Pat smiled. "Special Delivery Service – mission accomplished!"